Betty Rubble

Barney Rubble

Baby Puss

Bamm-Bamm

The Flintstone family is back, and Fred Flintstone has a new hobby – fishing. But things don't go quite as he expects...

British Library Cataloguing in Publication Data
Grant, John, *1930-*
    Fred the fisherman.
    I. Title   II. Davies, Robin, *1950-*   III. Series
    823'.914 [J]
    ISBN 0-7214-1219-X

First edition

Published by Ladybird Books Ltd Loughborough Leicestershire UK
Ladybird Books Inc Auburn Maine 04210 USA

Printed in England

THE FLINTSTONES

in
Fred the Fisherman

by JOHN GRANT
illustrated by ROBIN DAVIES

Ladybird Books

Fred watched from the window as the postman turned into the street where the Flintstones lived. As soon as he saw him, Fred rushed outside. "Have you got any parcels for me? Fred Flintstone?" he shouted.

The postman handed him two packages. One was long and thin. The other was small and square. Fred hurried round the end of the house, and out of sight of prying eyes he undid the wrappings.

"At last!" he cried. "YABBA-DABBA-DOO!"

The long, thin package contained three
pieces of wood. When Fred fixed them
together, they made a slender fishing rod.
In the square package there was a box,
and an instruction book. Fred tipped out the
contents of the box. There was a spool of
fishing line, hooks of different sizes, a bundle
of brightly coloured feathers, and a lot of
odds and ends that Fred didn't recognise.

Fred tiptoed round to the kitchen window to see what Wilma was doing. She was speaking on the telephone to Betty Rubble. "Good!" said Fred to himself. "She won't bother me for at least an hour!"

Then he went back to his new fishing tackle and sat down. Soon he was hard at work, mumbling to himself and checking the book at each step. At last he sat back, very pleased.

"Hi, there, Fred!" came Barney's cheery voice. He was leaning over the garden wall. "What are you doing?"

"Hello, Barney," Fred called back. "You are witnessing a great moment in the life of F Flintstone, Esquire. What do you think this is?"

"It looks like a fishing rod to me," said Barney.

"Quite!" said Fred. "But not just *any* fishing rod. I have taken up fly fishing!"

"What do you do with the flies once you've caught them?" asked Barney. "They're a bit small to eat!"

"I will use flies to catch fish," said Fred. "I made this fly myself. Flintstone Fancy, I'm going to call it. What sort of fish do you think this will catch?"

"Stupid ones, if they think that's a fly," replied Barney. "I'm a bent pin and worm man myself."

"Bent pin and worm!" said Fred, scornfully. "Come fishing with me and you'll see *real* fishing!"

Wilma came to join them. "We'll all go," she said. "Betty too. We'll have a picnic. Bamm-Bamm and Pebbles will like that."

"That's all right by me," said Fred. "Just remember one thing. Fly fishing is a delicate art. I don't want people running and jumping and shouting up and down the river bank."

And so it was arranged that the Flintstones and the Rubbles would have a riverside picnic on the following Saturday.

As soon as breakfast was over on Saturday, Fred and Barney loaded their families into their cars and set off for the river. It was a tight squeeze, because the food for the picnic took up a lot of room. Fred was afraid his precious fly rod might be damaged and he watched anxiously as everyone got in. Dino wanted to come too, but there was really no room for him. Fred promised to bring him home some extra special fish for his supper.

The picnic place was a sunny clearing a little way from the river. Betty and Wilma unloaded the picnic things, and Fred and Barney set off for the river to fish.

Bamm-Bamm wanted to go too. Pebbles had a new skipping rope, however, and Wilma and Betty said that all the girls would stay behind and have fun together. So Bamm-Bamm trotted after Fred and Barney.

Barney and Bamm-Bamm sat on a log and
watched Fred get ready. Frowning, and with
his tongue sticking out, Fred fastened his
Flintstone Fancy artificial fly to the end of the
fishing line. Then he stepped up to the
water's edge. He waggled the rod back and
forward a few times above his head, then he
gave a quick flick.

The line whirled round and over his head, and he gave a loud yell. The hook had caught him by the ear.

Fred muttered for a moment, rubbing his sore ear. Then he tried again. The line didn't fly over his head this time. It just hung from the end of the rod in a great tangle. Fred began to undo the tangle carefully.

"Can I help, Fred?" asked Barney.

"Yes!" said Fred. "By going somewhere else. I can't concentrate with people watching."

"Come on, Bamm-Bamm," said Barney. "We'll find our own place, and leave Uncle Fred in peace. I've got a can of lovely worms."

Fred waited until their footsteps faded in the distance. Then he finished straightening out the tangled line, took out his instruction book and began reading. He held it in one hand and his fishing rod in the other. He flicked and waved the rod above his head, checking the book as he did so.

Then he put the book away and turned back to the river.

Taking a deep breath, Fred flicked his line once more. And it was perfect! Just like the diagram in the book. There was only one thing wrong. Instead of flying straight out and landing in the water, the Flintstone Fancy caught the leaves of an overhanging tree branch… and stuck fast!

Barney meantime was having great luck. Bamm-Bamm jumped up and down and shouted with delight every time Barney landed another fat fish. "I think that's enough, Bamm-Bamm," said Barney. "Let's go and see how Uncle Fred is doing."

"Whatever are you doing, Fred?" cried Barney, as they came along the bank.

Fred was clinging to the tree branch, trying to reach the line caught in the leaves. The branch was bending… and Fred was slipping!

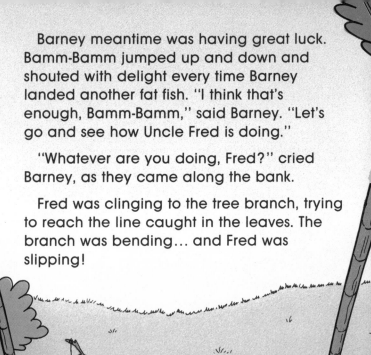

"Don't move, Fred!" cried Barney. He dashed back to the picnic place.

Wilma and Betty were setting out the food for the picnic when Barney rushed up and grabbed Pebbles' skipping rope. "I need this for Fred!" he shouted, and ran off again.

"Don't tell me that Fred's given up fishing for skipping!" said Wilma. "I think we'd better go and see what he's up to."

They arrived in time to see Barney climbing up to tie one end of the skipping rope to the tip of a long, slender tree growing out over the river. He threw the other end to Fred.

"Tie it round you, Fred!" he cried. "It's a safety line."

"Thanks," gasped Fred, struggling to tie the rope with one hand.

At last he managed it... but at the same moment he lost his balance and fell off the branch.

"Oh, dear!" cried Wilma. "He'll get wet!"

But he didn't. With a jerk he stopped, bobbing up and down over the water as the tree sprang up and down with his weight.

"I'm coming, Fred!" cried Barney. "Hang on!"

"There's nothing else I *can* do!" Fred shouted back. But before Barney could do anything, Bamm-Bamm was there first. His Uncle Fred was in trouble. He would save him!

Bamm-Bamm wrapped his small arms around the tree and heaved. And Fred found himself whipped into the air. Then back again as the tree sprang back. But Bamm-Bamm wasn't giving up. The tree whipped to and fro. Fred bounced up and down.

"Hi, Fred," shouted Barney. "You look like a worm on a fishing line!"

Just as Barney spoke an enormous fish leapt from the river, snapping at Fred. Fred let out a yell, and Bamm-Bamm heaved again. And the fish leapt again.

"Maybe the fish is just being playful," said Betty.

"Licking its lips?" cried Fred. "Do something, somebody!"

At that moment, Barney's knot came loose from the tree. As the fish made another grab, Fred landed on it, and they both disappeared with an enormous splash.

Bamm-Bamm picked up the loose end of the skipping rope, put it over his shoulder and dragged Fred into shallow water.

Fred was clutching the fish.

The others helped him out of the river and up the bank. By this time, the Flintstone Fancy had come free from the leaves. Fred gathered up his fishing tackle, then he and Barney between them carried the fish back to the picnic place.

As the Flintstones and the Rubbles sat down to their picnic, Barney said, "Well, Fred, I don't mind admitting... that fish of yours is bigger than any fish *I* ever caught."

"I'm so proud of you," said Wilma.

Fred had fully recovered from his adventure. He held up the Flintstone Fancy artificial fly. "Fly fishing is an art. A science. It's not for just anybody."

"Fred old buddy," said Barney, "I'm going to stick to my bent pin and can of worms. As far as I can see, fly fishing is far too dangerous."